OWL
AND OTHER
SCRAMBLES

LISL WEIL

A Unicorn Book • E. P. Dutton   New York

Library of Congress Cataloging in Publication Data

Weil, Lisl.   Owl and other scrambles.
(A Unicorn book)

Summary: Includes picture words for each letter of
the alphabet which are partially composed of the letters
that spell the name of the item when unscrambled.
[1. Picture puzzles. 2. Alphabet] I. Title.
PZ7.W4330w 1980 [E] 80-13742 ISBN: 0-525-36527-3

Published in the United States by E. P. Dutton, a Division
of Elsevier-Dutton Publishing Company, Inc., New York

Published simultaneously in Canada by Clarke,
Irwin & Company Limited, Toronto and Vancouver

Editor: Emilie McLeod   Designer: Stacie Rogoff

Printed in the U.S.A.   First Edition
10 9 8 7 6 5 4 3 2 1

to

sharing good times and laughter

Introduction

Think of a lion. Think of the shapes of the letters that spell LION and the lion's shape. Lisl Weil uses the letters to draw a lion.

It's not the easiest way to spell, and the letters get scrambled, but it's fun.

Each word makes a picture-puzzle with its own clues. There is one or more scramble for each letter in the alphabet. Some are easy, some are hard. But the words are all spelled out in the back of this book. They are arranged alphabetically in the order of their beginning letter.

ÁBCDEFGHIJKLM

ABĊDEFGHIJKLM

NOPQRSTUVWXYZ

ABCDEFGHIJKLM

NOPQRSTUVWXYZ

ABCDĖḞGHIJKLM

NOPQRSTUVWXYZ

ABCDEFĠHIJKLM

NOPQRSTUVWXYZ

ABCDEFGHIJKLM

NOPQRSTUVWXYZ

ABCDEFGHİJKLM

NOPQRSTUVWXYZ

ABCDEFGHIJKĹḾ

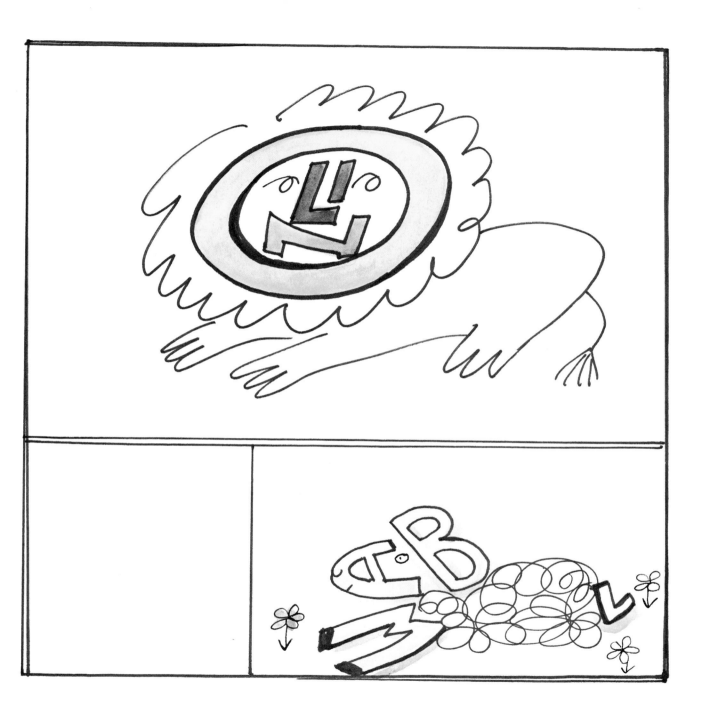

NOPQRSTUVWXYZ

ABCDEFGHIJKLM

NOPQRSTUVWXYZ

ABCDEFGHIJKLM

ÑÒÓPQRSTUVWXYZ

ABCDEFGHIJKLM

ABCDEFGHIJKLM

NOPQRSTUVWXYZ

ABCDEFGHIJKLM

NOPQRSTUVWXYŻ

Here are the PICTURE words unscrambled.

A	B	C	D	E
ANGEL APE AIRPLANE	BED BEE	CAB COOK CAT CLOWN	DOG DRAGON DOLL	ELEPHANT
F FROG	**G** GIANT GOOSE GNOME	**H** HORSE HOUSE	**I** IGLOO	**J** JUGGLER
K KANGAROO	**L** LION LAMB	**M** MERMAID MOUSE MAN	**N** NUTCRACKER	**O** OWL
P PIRATE	**Q** QUEEN	**R** REINDEER	**S** SNAIL	**T** TABLE TUB
U UMBRELLA	**V** VAN	**W** WITCH	**XY**	**Z** ZEBRA